Lost in the Desert

by

Elizabeth Kay

Illustrated by Dylan Gibson

For Bob

First published in 2011 in Great Britain by
Barrington Stoke Ltd
18 Walker St, Edinburgh, EH3 7LP

www.barringtonstoke.co.uk

Copyright © 2011 Elizabeth Kay
Illustrations © Dylan Gibson

The moral right of the author has been asserted in
accordance with the Copyright, Designs and
Patents Act 1988

ISBN: 978-1-84299-404-7

Printed in Great Britain by Bell & Bain Ltd

Contents

Chapter 1
Boot Camp

"You can't make me eat that," I said.

"I'm not even going to try," snapped Gary. "But you don't get anything else."

I wasn't going to let some idiot get the better of me, so I tipped my dinner on the floor. "You can't let me starve," I told him. "My mum and dad are paying a fortune for this place."

"You still haven't got it, have you, Max?" said Gary. "This isn't a holiday camp. This is Boot Camp in the Gobi Desert. You're here to learn some manners."

I kicked the plate across the floor of the tent. It left a trail of gravy behind it. Gary picked up a cloth, and threw it at me. "Clear it up," he said, dead nasty. "Clear it up, or you'll be here all night."

I don't think so, I said to myself. *You can't keep me here. There aren't any fences. There's nothing to stop me just going off into the sunset if I want to.*

"The last kid who tried to run away nearly died," said Gary, as if he'd read my mind. "There's nothing out there, Max. That's why Mongolia is such a good place for making selfish kids like you change your ways. There are no trees, no bushes – and no

water, unless you know where to look. Don't even think about it."

There were six of us stuck here, six of us with rich parents. We all saw more of our pets than we did our parents, and most of us got on better with them, too. I've got an African grey parrot called Ace. I've taught him to swear, and he's really good at it. Some of the other people here were OK. Some of them weren't. But I'm telling you, none of them were as hard as me.

I didn't clear up the mess. I just folded my arms and sat there. It got dark, and the stars came out.

"Hungry?" asked Gary.

"Not for that rubbish," I said. "I want a burger and chips. If I starve to death, you'll be in big trouble. Know what I'm saying?"

"You'll change your tune by the morning," said Gary. "Goodnight."

I didn't reply. I had other plans.

I knew I'd need something to eat and drink, so I crept into the kitchen and filled my pockets with chocolate bars and cans of Coke. I took Gary's red jacket, too, because it got cold at night, and my baseball hat. There wasn't any point taking my phone, because there wasn't any signal. Then I just walked out of there, and set off towards the mountains with a smile on my face.

Back home, I swim in our pool most days, so I'm in pretty good shape. I knew I could put in some miles before anyone missed me. By the time it started to get light I'd reached the foot-hills, so I used Gary's jacket as a pillow, and had a nap in the shelter of a rock.

Chapter 2
Escape

It was the noise that woke me up, like the roar of a motorway a long way off. Not that there was going to be any traffic out here – there weren't any roads. I opened my eyes. It didn't seem to be morning any more. The sky had gone a funny colour. The wind was throwing dirt around like a kid in a sand pit and I couldn't see the next rock, let alone the mountains. Going back to sleep seemed like a smart move, so I did.

When I woke up the next time, the wind had died away. I hurt in all sorts of places from lying on the rocky ground, and my mouth was so dry that my lips cracked when I took a drink. I looked at my watch, but sand had got in it and it had stopped.

I could see the mountains again now, so I ate another chocolate bar, and started walking. I'd show them. They wouldn't expect me to get this far. It was all uphill now, but I didn't mind that. Before long I'd be high enough to see all the way back to where the camp was. I might even be able to see people moving about, like ants. I waited until I thought I was high enough before I turned round to look.

I couldn't see a single one of those round white tents we'd been sleeping in. Gers, they called them. I couldn't see anything except miles and miles of nothing.

I couldn't believe it. I was so shocked I looked up at the sky instead. It was less scary.

Up in the sky, a huge eagle was flying in a lazy circle above me. I like birds – they don't act as if they're your best friend the way dogs do. I once found a pigeon with a broken wing. I put a stiff wooden splint on its wing, just like I'd seen a vet do on TV, and after a few weeks it got better. I watched it fly away.

I wished I could fly away, because I was beginning to think I might have done something very, very stupid.

I ate the rest of the chocolate, and started to walk. I didn't see anyone or anything all day, and every so often, when I let myself think about it, I felt a jolt of pure fear. By the time it was dark I'd finished all the Coke, and I was so tired I could hardly stand up. I found

another rock and lay down under it, but I had this horrible feeling that once I fell asleep I would never wake up again.

Everything got a bit dreamy after that. I remember feeling cold, and wishing I was back home, and then hearing all these silly voices. Trying to work out what they were saying. Opening my eyes, and seeing the devil himself – this horrible hairy face, barely two inches from my own. He had horns on his head, and a beard on his chin, and eyes like yellow slits. He smelt bad, too. I tried to tell him to go away, and found out that I couldn't speak because my throat had closed up. My head hurt, too.

I remember wondering if this was what it was like to die.

Chapter 3
Zul

Someone was pushing something wet against my lips. After a moment or two I worked out it was a bottle of water, so I drank and drank. The bottle was being held by a girl with black hair and slanting eyes. She said something, but I couldn't understand her.

"I'm English," I croaked, because I've got black hair too and she might have thought I was Mongolian. The dreamy feeling was going away, and I realised that the hairy face I'd seen before hers had belonged to a large ginger goat.

"English?" she repeated.

She wasn't that old, just a few years younger than me maybe. She was wearing a blue jumper, and she had a little string of beads round her neck.

"What are you doing here?" she asked.

I was so surprised that she spoke English that I didn't reply.

"Hungry?"

I nodded.

She put her hand into her pocket, and handed me something that smelt like cheese. I ate some of it and I felt a bit better.

"What are you doing here?" she said again.

"I got lost."

She gave me a funny look. "How can you get lost when the sky is full of stars? They are like a map."

Normally, I'm really quick with the chat. But this time, I couldn't think of a single thing to say.

"My name is Zul," she said. "What is your name?"

"Max. How come you speak such good English?"

"I go to school, of course," she said. "I love school. We get people from other countries who come to teach us, and then go home again. Chinese. Russian. And for the last three years, English. Can you ride?"

I realised she had her hand looped through the reins of a grey horse. "Of course I can," I said. I'd only had a few lessons, but I wasn't going to tell *her* that.

"Get up behind me, then," she said.

She swung herself up into the horse's saddle. It took me three goes to climb up behind her. The reins were really long, and she whirled them round her head like a lasso to get the goats to go where she wanted. There were about twenty of them, all different colours and sizes. We set off after them, but as soon as the horse started to trot I fell off.

"I thought you said you could ride?" she said.

"Give me a break. I've been without food or water for two days."

She didn't reply – but her face told me that she didn't think that was the real reason, and that only an idiot would get lost in the Gobi Desert without food or water.

Chapter 4
The Wolf

We rode for a while over flat, stony ground, and it started to get dark. Zul said, "We can spend the night at a ger I passed this morning."

I couldn't remember what a ger was, so I suppose I looked a bit blank.

"A ger," she said. "Tent. House."

"I know what a ger is," I lied. "Do you know the people who live there, then?"

17

"No."

I thought about knocking on the door of people I'd never met before, and expecting them to put me up. "How do you know we'll be welcome?" I asked.

She turned round to look at me. "What do you mean?"

"They may not have room."

"Of course they will have room. Everyone has room for travellers. They will have dogs, too, which is good because – "

And, bang on cue, a dog started howling in the distance.

"That's good, isn't it?" I said. "It means we're not too far away."

"That is not a dog," she said. "It is a wolf."

No one at the boot camp had said anything about wolves. It had to be a joke. I do a good howl, so I lifted my face to the moon and did my impression of a wolf.

"Shut *up*," she hissed. "Wolves are dangerous. There was a girl, about my age. She sent a text to her mother to say that the bus had dropped her off at the end of the track and she was walking back, but she never got home. The wolves ate her."

"Yeah, right," I said.

She shook her head, as if I was crazy.

I suddenly realised she hadn't been joking.

Just as suddenly as it had started to howl, the wolf went quiet again. The silence was creepy. I didn't like it. It felt like a setting for a horror film. We rode on, but we didn't hear it again.

I was really glad when I saw the pale shape of the ger in the distance, and smelt the smoke from its metal cooking stove. I took off my baseball hat, and ran a hand through my hair. It was full of sand.

"Leave your hat on," said Zul. "It is bad manners to take it off."

Gary had said I was out here to learn some manners. I smiled. I don't think they were the sort of manners he'd meant.

To my surprise there was a solar panel outside the ger, and a satellite dish. A boy took Zul's horse. His parents showed us indoors, sat us down and gave us bowls of hot milk. The milk was followed by something that was white and rubbery.

"That's urum," said Zul. "Dried cream."

"You're joking."

"*Eat it*," she hissed. "They don't have much food."

So I ate all of it, and it was OK. It was followed by meat, in a sort of soup. It was only when I'd finished it that I remembered the dinner I'd tipped on the floor at the camp, and I felt a bit ... I don't know ... bad, I suppose.

We had a bed each. When I thought about the night I'd spent on the ground it was the best bed ever, and I fell asleep right away.

Chapter 5
The Plane

The next morning we got up as soon as it was light. We had some more milk and a sort of meat pie, and then we went outside. Two horses were standing there, with saddles on. One of them was Zul's grey mare. The other one was black.

"They are lending you a horse," said Zul.

I couldn't believe it. A horse had to be worth a lot of money. It was like saying to some kid you'd never met before, "Here, take my bike. I'll pick it up next month."

"We can go much faster with two horses," said Zul. She turned her grey mare round, and galloped off after the ginger goat.

He was trouble, that one. He was either fighting with one of the other goats, or trying to get away. Zul didn't even hold on with her hands, and she leaned so far over to flick him with her reins that I couldn't understand how she was able to stay on at all. She was the best rider I'd ever seen. I didn't tell her I'd never galloped.

By midday it was really hot. When we stopped at a well for a drink, there were flies everywhere. To fend them off, the horses nodded their heads and swished their tails. We had a rest, and something to eat. Then we got going again.

It was mid-afternoon when I heard the plane. It sounded so out of place. All I'd heard for the past few hours had been flies, goats, horses, and Zul's voice shouting, "Shoo! Shoo!" to make the animals go where she wanted. Otherwise, there was total silence. I liked the silence. It felt good, in a way I can't explain. I looked up. It wasn't a big plane, and it was flying quite low.

And then it hit me. It was looking for *me*.

All at once, I knew I didn't want to be found. Not yet. The day before, when I'd had nothing to eat or drink that's exactly what I'd wanted, but now ... I looked round. There was nowhere to hide. No trees, no bushes, nothing. Zul was watching the plane, as if it was something she'd hardly ever seen before. I suddenly thought, she's not really that different from the people who lived here thousands of years ago, riding horses and herding goats. But then I thought – she's

wearing jeans, just like mine. Trainers. A jumper. Our hair's even the same colour. I could be her older brother.

The plane's engine was getting louder; it was coming closer for a better look. Just in time I thought of Gary's bright red jacket. I took it off, and turned it inside out. The plane passed overhead, then it started to climb again and before long it had gone.

Chapter 6
Zul's Ger

Zul gave me a funny look.

"Yes, all right," I said. "I know that plane was looking for me. But I don't want to go back."

"Won't your parents be worried about you?"

"My parents?" I laughed. "My parents don't have the *time* to worry about me."

"What do you mean? Everybody's day has the same number of hours."

"My father spends all day at meetings. My mother spends all day shopping."

"*Shopping?*" Zul stared at me. "How can shopping take up a whole day?"

I didn't really know that myself, so I said, "Won't your parents be worried about *you?*"

"Only if I don't get the goats home tonight. They will not know about the wolf. Wolves normally live further west." She spotted the ginger goat straying away from the herd again, so she dashed off after him at full gallop.

I'd never met a girl like Zul. I didn't want her thinking I was useless.

We reached her parents' ger at sunset. Her father had heard us coming, and he was standing outside, waiting for us.

He was wearing a dress.

In the past, I'd have made some joke about it, but Zul's father didn't look like someone you made fun of. The dress nearly went down to his feet, and at the end of his sleeves he had bright blue cuffs. He wore an orange sash tied round his waist, and thick leather boots, and a wicked sheath knife was tucked into his sash. He looked like he knew how to use it, as well. We went inside. Zul's little brother ran over to her and hugged her. He had a really stupid name – Bat.

Zul talked very fast, and her father nodded every so often. Although I'd seen a solar panel and a satellite dish at the other ger, Zul's one didn't have them. So there was no TV, no phone, and no computer. The only

way her father could send a message to anyone was by riding to the next ger on horseback. And he wasn't about to do that, because Zul's mother had gone to the hospital in the nearest town to have a baby. He wasn't going to leave an eleven-year-old girl in charge of both her little brother *and* the animals, was he? He wouldn't do that.

The next morning, Zul poked me in the ribs and said, "You are going to help me milk the goats. But don't go near the ginger one, because he has a nasty temper."

"I'm not milking anything," I said. "I'm going back to sleep."

"Oh no you're not," she hissed. "Because after we have seen to the goats, my father is going to take you to his brother's ger. They have a satellite dish there, and they can ring the police who will take you back to your hotel."

"And leave you in charge?"

"It will only be for half a day."

I was going to have to tell the truth.

Chapter 7
The Accident

"I wasn't staying in a hotel," I said. "I ran away from the Gobi Boot Camp."

Zul just stared at me. Then she said, "I might have guessed. Even *I* have heard of *that* place. The sooner you go back, the better. You are rubbish."

Nobody calls me rubbish and gets away with it, but Zul had gone before I could reply. So I got dressed, and went outside. Zul's father handed me a bucket, and pointed to a big grey goat. I took the bucket. I didn't dare do anything else.

I couldn't get it right. All the goats had sharp horns, and they all thought that butting someone who was milking one of their mates was the best joke in the world. It wasn't like the pictures you see of people milking cows. I didn't have a stool. I had to sit back on my heels, which was hard. I fell over five times, and kicked over the bucket.

Zul's little brother Bat came out, and tried to show me how to do it. I wasn't going to be told what to do by a little kid, so I pushed him out of the way. I didn't see the ginger goat with the nasty temper behind me until it was too late. The goat butted Bat so hard that the kid flew up in the air, and landed with his arm twisted beneath him.

He screamed, and burst into tears. His arm was all wrong – twisted in an S-shape. Both Zul and her father came running. I knew Bat's arm was broken. I'd seen it all before, only that time it had been the wing of a bird.

Zul gave me a long hard look. "What happened?"

I told her. I felt really bad. Bat wasn't a bad little kid, and he'd tried to help me.

Zul looked furious. "My father will have to take him to hospital," she said. "On horse-back."

That was going to hurt. "Bat's arm needs to be held in place with a stiff wooden splint," I said. "I can do it. I've done it before."

"Yeah, right," she said, just the way *I* had when she'd told me about the wolf.

"I'm telling you the truth," I said.

"Why should I believe you?"

"Because I'm really really sorry," I said. It felt odd, saying that. *Sorry* wasn't a word I used. But Bat was still crying, and I felt like joining him. "We need a bit of wood," I said. "And some strips of cloth."

Zul's father put a saddle on his horse, while I played doctor. I was very gentle, and when I'd finished Bat gave me a watery smile. Once the pieces of bone stopped moving against one another, it didn't hurt quite as much.

When Bat and his dad had gone Zul turned to me and said, "You do realise what this means, don't you?"

"What?"

"The two of us are going to have to do everything for the next few days. Milk the goats, make the cheese curds, water the horses."

I took a deep breath. "Right," I said. "Let's get started."

Chapter 8
The Dog from Hell

And so I became a herds-man. It was hard work, but my riding got better very quickly, and I learned to milk the goats properly. We had no TV or computer games or iPods, so in the evenings Zul would try to teach me the song that was their number one at the time. It was called, would you believe it, "My Mother Makes Tea". Other popular songs were about wild horses, and flying eagles. They were so different to the songs I knew, which were mainly about being fed up with life. *Everything* out here was different. Cleaner. Quieter. Friendlier. Zul wanted to know what it was like, living in a city, so I told her. Dirty, noisy, and smelly.

That night we heard the wolf again.

"It will be winter soon," said Zul. "That is when wolves are most dangerous."

I thought she meant that wolves were dangerous because they had less to eat in the winter. I didn't realise she meant they were dangerous for a completely different reason.

We didn't see the plane again. Each afternoon Zul and I took the goats and a small herd of horses to the well. We had to pump the water into a metal trough, and it was hard work. The horses always drank first, and then the goats.

On the fifth day the horses suddenly pricked up their ears. Then they started to move about, and whinny to each other. I looked round, and saw that a strange dog had appeared on the skyline. For one horrible moment I thought it was the wolf, because Zul looked really scared, and she wasn't someone who scared easily. The dog was behaving very oddly. Its ears were laid back, and it was snapping at thin air and weaving to and fro like it was drunk.

The horses bolted – just left, in a cloud of dust.

"Stay with goats, Max!" yelled Zul. "And keep them away from that dog!" She dashed off after the horses, leaning low in the saddle. But even though she was a brilliant horse-woman, I didn't think she'd catch up with them that fast because none of them were carrying the weight of a saddle and a rider.

The goats were getting restless now, and the dog was walking slowly towards us. It was showing its teeth, and it was snarling in a really nasty way. And then I saw it was drooling, and, all of a sudden, I knew why Zul had been so scared.

The dog was sick – it had rabies.

I remember some idiot in my class once asking what the cure for rabies was. There isn't one, of course. If you get bitten and you get ill, you die. Unless you can get the right injection within 24 hours, and the chances of that out here were nil.

I felt an icy trickle of sweat at the back of my neck. Dying from rabies is a horrible death; you see monsters in your head and you're desperately thirsty but you can't drink. Perhaps the dog had caught it from the wolf – because if the wolf we'd heard had been sick, it explained why it wasn't with its pack, further west.

And then I heard something I hadn't heard for ages – the sound of a truck. If it was someone from round here they'd know what to do. They might even have a gun, because the dog wasn't ever going to get better, and the kindest thing was to kill it. I turned to look – and to my horror I saw one of the grey buses that had taken me to the camp coming towards me, through the dust.

Chapter 9
A Big Shock

Everything seemed to happen very slowly. The dog was still coming towards me, making odd little sounds that weren't proper barks. The goats were moving about, and the truck had slowed to a stop. To my surprise, I could see Zul's little brother Bat sitting in the back, next to a woman holding a baby. The first person to get out was Gary, the guy from the camp who'd wanted me to learn some manners. He didn't look happy. The second one was Zul's father. He must have met Gary in the town, when he took Bat to hospital. It wasn't a big town. And he'd told Gary where to find me.

But the real shock was my parents.

I just stared. My mother was wearing a long flowery skirt, lots of gold jewellery and a big floppy hat. My father was wearing a posh safari suit, and designer sunglasses.

"*Max!*" cried my mother, and she started to run towards me. It looked as if she'd been crying. Her make-up was all smudged.

The dog snapped at nothing again, and then it spotted her. Maybe it was the flowery skirt, or perhaps it was the tinkling of the bracelets. Whatever the reason, it was hate at first sight. The French call rabies *La Rage*, and I could see why. The dog was as mad as hell, and it wanted to rip her to pieces. It leaped forward, and ran straight at her.

I didn't stop to think. I turned my horse and shouted, "Shoo! Shoo!" The horse didn't want to go anywhere near the dog, but I was a much better rider than I had been a few days before. After tossing his head and dancing sideways he did as I asked, and in no time at all I was between the dog and my mother. The horse reared up, and one of his hooves hit the dog on the side of its head. The dog flew through the air, landed on its back behind the metal water trough, and lay still.

My mother just stood there, her mouth open, her skirt flapping around her in the wind.

My horse settled down once it couldn't see the dog any more.

A group of horses without riders appeared on the skyline, followed by Zul. She spotted the dog, drew her hand across her throat and

gave me a thumbs-up. It was her way of telling me that the dog really was dead, and out of its misery.

"Oy!" bellowed Gary. "Max! You're in big, big trouble."

"I don't think so," said my father.

I wondered if he had been crying as well, because he wiped his eyes at least twice with the back of his hand.

"I know a rabid dog when I see one," he said. "He may have just saved his mother's life."

I didn't know what to say, which was a first as far as me and my dad were concerned.

Zul cantered over. "This is your *mother*?" she said.

I nodded. "And that's my dad." Right at that moment I wished the ground would open up and swallow me. They were the most embarrassing parents ever.

"They will be more than welcome to eat at our ger," said Zul.

"But ..."

"They are your *parents*," hissed Zul. "Whatever you think of the strange way they dress, you should show them some respect." Then she saw her own father, and after that the truck and the rest of the passengers. "That's *my* mother!" she shrieked at the top of her voice. "And she's had the baby!"

Chapter 10
A Change of Heart

Zul and I rode back to the ger, driving the goats and the horses in front of us. Everyone else followed in the bus. Zul kept saying how pleased she was that she now had a sister. I reckoned that if the new sister was anything like Zul, she'd have her hands full.

When my dad arrived at the ger, he took off his hat.

"Put it back on," I hissed. "It's bad manners to take it off."

He gave me a funny look, but he did as I asked.

Zul told her father about everything we'd done as the two of them handed out cups of milk and urum. Then Zul's father started to speak, and Zul translated what he said. He told my parents how I had learned to milk the goats, and take the horses to water, and helped Zul with her English. He thanked them for the loan of their son, and told them how he hoped *his* son would grow up to be just like me.

Gary's face was a picture. He looked as though he was about to tell them how awful I'd been – then he seemed to change his mind.

"I want to say something," said Zul, when her father stopped talking. "I used to think I wanted to live in a city, because life sounded much more exciting. I know now that it is not. You do not have time for anything. You do not even have time for Max." She took a deep breath. "I know I should not speak like this to older people, but sometimes rules have to be broken. Max broke *your* rules because it was the only way to get you to take notice of him."

Nobody spoke for a moment. Then my mum said, "We do care, Zul. That's why we're out here. When we heard Max was missing we dropped everything, and came."

"We're going to make some changes," my dad added. "We haven't had a holiday together as a family for years. We've always been too busy. But now we're out here, we thought ... there's so much to see." He turned to Zul. "If your father could spare you, we'd like you to come along as well."

Zul spoke very rapidly to her father so that all the words ran together. He thought for a moment, and then answered her.

"He says that my mother's sister is coming here tomorrow to help with the baby," Zul told us. "If I want to come with you, I can."

"We could fly," I said. "Would you like that?"

"In a plane? So that I can see the desert from the air, like an eagle?"

"Just like an eagle," I said, because birds are great.

"I think I'm out of a job," said Gary. But he was smiling. I looked at my dad.

He grinned at me.

And I grinned back.

AUTHOR ID

Name: Elizabeth Kay

Likes: Snow, animals, travel.

Dislikes: Bony fish and bad drivers.

3 words that best describe me:
Arty, funny, energetic.

A secret not many people know:
I hated maths at school.

ILLUSTRATOR ID

Name: Dylan Gibson

Likes: Going out, walks, cycling, reading.

Dislikes: Sundays and Monday mornings!

3 words that best describe me:
Tall, talkative and hard-working.

A secret not many people know:
I hate flying!

Barrington Stoke would like to thank all its readers for commenting on the manuscript before publication and in particular:

Jamie Boyd
Charlie Brett
Eilidh Buchan
Hannah Doyle
Carly Gower
Mrs Harvey
Gemma Hollis
Neave Johnson
Dylan King
Aimee McVicars
Ewan Melville
Aimee Miller
Serena Naismith
Kyle Rennie
Jamie-Lee Steel
James Wilson
Leanne Woolsey

Become a Consultant!

Would you like to be a consultant? Ask your parent, carer or teacher to contact us at the email address below – we'd love to hear from them! They can also find out more by visiting our website.

schools@barringtonstoke.co.uk
www.barringtonstoke.co.uk